Tales from the CANYONS of the DAMNED

PRESENTED BY USA TODAY BESTSELLING AUTHOR

DANIEL ARTHUR SMITH

Tales from the Canyons of the Damned 43

Special thanks to editor Jessica West

  First Edition ISBN: 978-1-946777-82-9

Cover By Daniel Arthur Smith

Other Horror Fiction from Holt Smith ltd
Agroland
Tower
Attack of the Kung Fu Mummies

For Susan, Tristan, & Oliver, as all things are.

Someplace Wonderful
Ernie Howard

They found Tess Jenkins's daughter in the snow that day without a stitch of clothing on her. Doc Holston said the girl wasn't even shivering when the search party found her. But doc also said that that was what happens in the last stages of hypothermia. I guess that's true. You would probably know better than me, but Wendy Jenkins wasn't in the last stages of hypothermia. Randy Dunmore was the one who initially found her, and he told me that when he touched the girl's shoulder it had been like touching a damn furnace.

"The damn snow was melted all around her, Charlie, and she was smiling like it was a sunny day in June," Randy said.

We didn't say much after that. One of the reasons being that we were both around the same age and talking about much of anything didn't come naturally to us. The other was I think neither of us wanted to face the fact that the Jenkins girl had been out in the wilderness for two weeks, naked as a jaybird. How in the hell did she survive that long? I reckon I know now. Boy do I ever. I asked Randy if she said anything to him when he found her.

"I asked where she'd been. She looked up at the sky and said, 'Someplace wonderful.' There was something wrong about that girl, Charlie. I was glad when the EMTs and her momma showed up," he said. That Randy Johnson, hmm...always the skittish type.

I lived next door to Tess and her daughter, and knew both of them pretty well. I had watched Wendy grow up into a gangly teenager and then to an almost full-grown woman. And Tess, I'd taken out a couple of times. And I know what you're going to ask me.

You weren't romantically involved with Mrs. Jenkins?

No, Sheriff Green. We were just friends. If you're trying to go with a crime of passion angle here, you're going down the wrong street.

Charlie, I already told you, You aren't being accused of anything.

Well, good on you then.

I took Tess out after her husband Harold passed a few years ago. Just to get her out of the house. We'd been neighbors for upwards of fifteen years, and I figured taking her out to dinner to get her mind on something else was the neighborly thing to do. I'm going to get to all the particulars of why I think they disappeared. It's nothing that you could ever imagine. You have to hear the full story first. That girl is the brightest and you might say scariest thing to come to Highland Falls in a dog's age. All I ask is that you hear me out and then you can judge for yourself. It won't take long, fellas.

Anyway, that girl only stayed in the hospital for one night of observation. I mean, I know there are ways to survive in the wilderness, but this was a sixteen-year-old cheerleader, not a bearded survivalist. She was gone for two weeks. Hell, even *you* stopped calling it a search and rescue and changed the goal to just seeing if we could find the poor girl's remains. I'm going off the rails a little bit. Back to the story.

Tess brings that girl home after her one-day stay at the hospital and a week goes by without incident. Then Tess is knocking on my door. She looked halfway between the realm of the living and the dead. Her hair was matted with sweat and god knew what else, and I caught a whiff of her when a slight breeze wandered by. She smelled like she hadn't seen water and a bar of soap in quite some time. I had to fight back my breakfast. I was stunned at how out of sorts she looked. Tess was the kind of lady who never went outside unless her face was made up. I feel bad that I judged her now. I probably would have looked the same way she did, knowing what she knew at that moment.

And what was that, Charlie?

That everything was going to change for everything and everyone. Can… Can I continue?

Please do, Charlie.

She looked at me with bloodshot eyes that had deep purple circles under them. "Can I come in, Charlie?"

I stood there staring at her for a second, thinking about the time I'd taken her out and how different that woman was from the woman standing before me. She asked me again and I snapped out of the shock.

I opened the door for her and got her inside as quickly as possible. I didn't want Mrs. Sanders down the street getting any ideas and telling half the town that Charlie Babbitt and Tess Jenkins were jumping into bed together. I wasn't going to have any of that even if Tess was offering. Oh how things have changed.

This was two days ago, right? I just want to have it right in my notes, Charlie.

Yes, sir. Two days. I think you'll see that things escalated very quickly after Tess started talking. Are we good with dates and particulars, now? I'd like to get this story out while it's still fresh in my mind. Because there is still lots to do.

I'll take the nod as a yes.

When I say that Tess smelled like she rolled around in a dead animal's cave, that isn't describing the experience as well as I can. The smell also had a wrongness to it, like an underlying chemical smell or a burnt electrical cord. The scent was giving me a headache, so I opened one of the front windows in the living room. I watched as she slowly sat down on my couch, and tried not to wince. I knew I'd have to fumigate that damn expensive piece of furniture afterward. That line of thought seems so stupid to me now...

Mr. Babbitt?

Oh yeah. Sorry.

So, Tess sits right down about as close as you are to me right now. She looked around the room like she'd never been in my house before. You know, like when people are sizing the room up. She turns her stare towards me, and I know the person I see before me isn't all there anymore. It was as if her eyes were seeing something totally different than just ole Charlie Babbitt in front of her.

"Wendy isn't right," she said.

"Not right how, Tess?" I said.

The room felt like it'd dropped a few degrees as we were sitting there. To the point where I could feel goosebumps on my forearms.

"She isn't here anymore. She's gone." Her voice sounded very monotone, like she was one of those automatic voices when you call someone's cell and they don't pick up. I remember the sound of it quite well because the next words out of her mouth were in complete contrast to the robotic voice.

"She's gone! And she's never coming back. Nothing is ever coming back. It changed her in the woods and now it's changing me! It's going to take me to the place."

Tess's voice made me want to jump out of my skin. I didn't know vocal cords could do such a thing. Go from nothing to screaming in two seconds.

Either there was something wrong with my memory or Tess was even more nuts than she was acting. Because earlier that morning, when I was eating breakfast, I'd seen Wendy in their back yard standing in the middle of it all and looking up at the sky. I'd thought nothing of it and simply finished my bran muffin. And now this woman sitting in my living room was telling me her daughter was gone once again.

"Where has she gone?" I said, not liking how shaky my voice was.

She turned to me and, with the creepiest smile on her face and in the most monotone voice, said, "Someplace wonderful. Go see for yourself."

It was as if her brain had flipped a switch. No more agitation and yelling. In its place was a simple calm. I felt every icy cold tingle in my body all at once and shivered in my warm living room. My mother used to say one of those shivers meant you were being touched by the dead. After having Tess Jenkins in my house, I would say she was right. She raised one of her filthy hands and pointed towards her house. Her teeth looked yellow and old as she smiled.

Now, normally I would have just called you guys, but I won't bullshit you and say curiosity didn't get the best of me. Against my better judgement, I got up off of my La-Z-Boy and started walking toward the front of the house. I looked back at Tess as I was opening the door. Her smile was gone, and she had a vacant look like she was daydreaming about white sandy beaches.

I left the door to my house open. I figured the situation was way past whatever gossiping neighbors had to say, so I walked the short distance between our front doors. I looked up at Tess's house and I don't know how to explain it, but something was inviting about it. I had the sudden urge that the only place I wanted to be was in that house. I walked through their front door with a smile on my face that was instantly wiped off when I saw Wendy sitting on the floor cross-legged. The only light in the room was from the open door.

The feeling of yearning was still there, but now it had a friend in bald-faced fear. The girl looked at me and let out a cackle that the Wicked Witch of the West would have been proud of. My feet were cemented to the floor, and I didn't even move when the door slammed shut behind me. My legs decided to work once again after I realized I was in a room with a weird girl in darkness. I went to the front window and pushed the blinds aside. When I looked back, Wendy was no longer sitting where she had been. I looked around the room and I can actually say that I have never been more scared in my entire life.

I heard footsteps coming from upstairs and I couldn't stop the compulsion in me to go to where the noise was coming from. I took the stairs two at a time. By the time I got to the top, my heart was beating so fast from fear and exertion that I thought maybe I was going to drop dead right there. I looked to my left and saw that one of the bedroom doors was wide open. Wendy Jenkins stood inside of the door. Her head was tilted to one side like a dog does when they don't understand a sound they're hearing.

"Everything okay, Wendy?"

"Everything is wonderful, Mr. Babbitt. You'll see."

Her mouth started to open in a silent scream. It just kept opening and I looked inside. I saw the brightest sun I'd ever seen, and I saw something that no human was ever allowed to see, but I had been chosen to see it. Right before I blacked out, I knew that nothing would ever be the same.

You okay, Charlie?

Oh. Guess I drifted off for a second. You have to understand… Well, yes, I guess you will, shortly.

I woke up on the grass of my yard. I was changed. Do you hear me officer? I was changed for the better, and I knew that it was my job—no matter how scared I was—to change the rest of the world. Don't look at me like that. I know you think I'm talking gibberish, but I have never been more sure of something in my entire life. The great shift that is required to birth this new and powerful master into our unworthy world starts with us. Don't you see?

Well, we found Wendy again. Tess Jenkins wasn't the one who called the police. You're not being arrested, we just wanted to check you out Charlie, make sure you were all okay upstairs.

I'm not crazy, Sheriff. In fact, far from it. I have been enlightened and you will be too.

Sounds good, Charlie. You're free to go.

Do not mock me. For when you mock me, you mock the elder god! For I am his servant! We all are his feast!

Okay, Charlie. Calm down. What exactly have you seen?

What have I seen!

Charlie, there is no need to shout. This is a small room. I can hear you loud and clear.

You stupid little pipsqueak, I have seen the end and the beginning to everything. I have seen gods that wouldn't eat, but simply breathe you in because you are nothing more than a molecule on a breath of air. I have seen the change. What have I seen indeed.

Max, we have a situation here. Possible 5150.

Yes, bring Max in here, he needs to see this too. He needs to see someplace wonderful and meet his new god.

Charlie, sit down, or I'll have to… How are you doing that with your mouth? What is that? Is that…? Oh god, it's so bright. Oh…

Kingdom Come:
Aliens and Evil
Steve Oden

The Blind Bear listens attentively to an explanation of why alien visitors have made contact with one of the warring sides in the struggle between former slave toys and their human masters.

He's glad, this once, to be sightless. The whirling outer walls of the spaceship have made his scout snake and bodyguard, Adderlene, dizzy. She tries her best to maintain a coiled defensive posture, but the Bear can feel her wobbling slightly through the paw that rests on her muscular body.

They are seated across the conference table from a large rodent, apparently the head of a peace mission from outer space. Burl Sook has removed his robe and hood to reveal a long, smooth-haired gray body scarred by old wounds, including a broken back.

The medical prowess of the aliens seems far advanced. Sook's spine is fused with an exterior frame of alloy links—the visible hump under his robe—that apparently reconnects the broken vertebrae, providing a full range of motion. He has begun to share background history connecting the off-world visitors to the current struggles on earth.

"The moon colonies were established long before most of the adult human population on the home world died from addiction to the suicide drug," he reveals. "Millions of orphaned children were left in the care of living toys and biomechanical guardians. Others—tens of thousands—were sent to the colonies."

"We never knew the humans who created us had also begun to explore outer space," the Blind Bear admits.

Burl Sook nods. "Archival data was lost during an electromagnetic hurricane blast from the sun. This hastened collapse of human civilization, both here and on settlements established in the solar system."

Bear asks, "Where else besides Luna?"

"Mars, Venus, the asteroid belt...and there were several ill-fated attempts to reach beyond the solar system."

The supreme commander of the rebel toys and their allies shakes his fuzzy head in amazement.

"Let me back up a little," the rat says. "Decimated human society turned inward, focusing on maintenance of the species in the absence of parental wisdom. Child kingdoms arose, led by teenagers who sought, above all else, new sensory inputs and immediate satisfaction. A generation arose unlike any other, raised on emotionless technology and games of violence and bloodshed."

"We know this history very well, having lived most of it," concedes the Blind Bear. "Sentient and loyal, the toys and bio-mech protectors became slaves. Soon, we were nothing more than flesh-and-blood victims for their games and other cruelties."

"Ye-sss," hisses Adderlene, coiled protectively beside her leader.

The snake's sensor-and-weapons hood is fully extended, despite Burl Sook's guarantee of peaceful intent. "Many of my sss-iblings died to sss-atissfy the blood lust of the human mon-sssters!"

"What you don't know is that the suicide drug also made its way to Luna. From there, it was trafficked to the other settlements. Contact was lost with earth. Life-support systems began to break down. Entire colonies died...all the men, women and children, whether they were addicted to the drug or not," the rat reveals.

The bear's body language shows consternation.

"But where did you come from? How did you build this amazing spaceship and learn to operate it?"

The rat's long snout wiggles and his jaws open in a smile.

"An astute observation!"

He waves a paw, and the walls of the conference room turn opaque, then crystal clear. They are at the center of a slowly revolving control complex. At various stations, unnaturally large animals of all sorts monitor instruments, screens, and computers. Rats, dogs, cats, and monkeys are dressed in silver uniforms. Bipedal, the animals have hands on their upper limbs.

"Pardon the surprise," the rat says, gesturing at the vessel's diverse crew.

"You could say we are the sole survivors of the space colonies. In reality, what you see are genetically enhanced creatures developed for deep-space exploration in ships like this. Rather than endangering themselves, the humans continued an established protocol of launching lab animals into the Great Beyond in hopes they would send back valuable data before dying."

"It was just as cruel as turning living toys and bio-mechs into slaves and fodder for blood sport," a new voice declares.

The Bear's ears twitch toward a console around which several animals have gathered. They step aside to reveal a human youth. Male, dark-skinned, early teens, with a broad grin on his face.

Bear can't see him, but he feels Adderlene suddenly constrict, hears the hum of her weapon system powering up.

"Isss one of them!" she hisses. "A hoo-man."

When the survivors of Captain Alva's recon company begin to trickle back to the Banfeinni Brigade's staging area, they are bloody, footsore and furious. Most of their stealth recon vehicles are twisted metal junk, destroyed in the enemy's saturation bombardment. The number of dead and injured continues to mount.

Being lured into a trap is embarrassment enough. Having no chance to strike back—only take cover and wait to sneak away—besmirches the Celtic brigade's sterling reputation. Alva expects to be stripped of rank for the costly failure. She's surprised when her superiors frame the mission as an intelligence-gathering coup.

"I know your troops are seething over what happened," says Toy Soldier, the new rebel supreme commander, during their after-action briefing. "Soon, you will have the opportunity for payback. You Irish possess long memories, I am told, and never forego revenge when it's due."

Brigadier General Brigid, leader of the Banfeinni female warriors, points her chin toward Alva and reminds her of the importance of the intelligence obtained at the cost of brave lives. The young woman's face is sharp-planed like the blade of a hatchet, but her eyes betray no anger or disappointment in the leader of her recon unit.

"You did not fail! Don't get yourself into a mope over the losses. 'Tis a miracle any of ye returned, but the information you brought back is more valuable than gold."

Toy Soldier gestures at the ceiling-tall master monitor and clicks through the data.

"Our experts have completed a detailed analysis of what your patrol found inside the building before it was blown up," he says. "Extrapolating from the machinery, lab equipment, bodies of technicians and scientists, and sheer size of the complex, it is obvious the surviving child kingdoms have built or created a monstrous secret weapon, as large as it is deadly!"

He pushes a paper hard copy image across the table for Brigid and Alva to consider. They've seen it before. It suggests something fearful and evil.

"If any doubter wants to argue against our conclusions, they should be prepared to explain this anomaly…a giant footprint in which your recon warriors took shelter when the balloon went up."

Brigid adds, "Cap'n Alva, what ye don't know about are test results from traces of DNA recovered in the lab complex by that quick-thinking scout o' yours. What's her name, Corporal Maeve? She kept her wits and brought back proof that the kingdoms have a living weapon even Saint Patrick himself might fear."

Alva, a battle-seasoned teenager, stares at the footprint photo and shakes her head in denial.

"By all that's holy, it can't be. Not an Arach!"

The general and Toy Soldier share grins.

"Nay, not exactly an Irish dragon. More like a whopping big dinosaur," Brigid explains.

"How?"

"I stress, we have not seen the creature itself," says Toy Soldier, "but our estimates based on your recon squad's discovery indicate a living giant reptile, six to seven stories tall or more, probably immune to most conventional weaponry, and somehow controlled by a remote operator."

General Brigid's voice turns icy with hatred: "Aye, the old villain, Dr. Congesto! He likely created the beastie from one of his genetic experiments! We think the building your team scouted was the place it was birthed."

"We have assets who tell us Congesto has crawled from under his slimy rock and soon will meet with the child kingdom leaders to demonstrate his new weapon of mass destruction. No coincidence there, but we have a plan for interrupting his sales pitch," reveals Toy Soldier.

He stares into the eyes of the crestfallen company commander.

"Captain Alva, this is why we want your company immediately back in action. Your orders are to probe deep in the heart of enemy territory to extract a special unit tasked with sowing confusion and capturing kingdom leaders. I am optimistic Dr. Congesto might be part of the bag, if our timing is right. Your mission is to get them back safely to the river and into our hands."

"Sir, what about the Arach...I mean, o' course, the reptile monster?"

A slow faint smile curves the supreme commander's lips when he replies, "Let us worry about the dinosaur. We have a plan for making it extinct again."

Dolly Bright Eyes knows their quarters are bugged. This is why her girls chatter excitedly about the upcoming performance for assembled enemy leaders and key staff, while practicing dance routines and preparing their costumes. They flash and spin colorful oriental fans that are part of their performance, laughing and helping one another stretch and loosen up.

This is the last rehearsal before tonight's show. Count Thaddeus's pimply-faced major domo has explained the schedule: a leadership meeting about rejuvenated prosecution of the war against rebellious toys, followed by a sumptuous dinner, then their performance. Under hypnotic influence, he has also revealed details about the subterranean levels of the fortress where the event will be held.

The dancers manipulate their fans, reflecting light like colored mirrors. It's a form of secret communication, using perfectly timed flashes to form the dashes and dots of old-fashioned Morse code. There's no need for the dancers to speak. They simply appear to be practicing hand movements with the fans.

All eyes are on the Dolly Bright Eyes and her unit leaders. They go over the plan again, answer questions and update information about the fortress layout and escape routes.

"Timing depends on how long their strategy session lasts. I understand from the major domo there will be a vote about using the secret weapon. Even he does not know what sort of weapon had been developed. The discussion could go on for a long time. We've got to be flexible," she signals.

"Also, a new guilty party has been added to our list of war criminals. Dr. Congesto himself will be on hand. He apparently is selling the new weapon, and there could be protracted debate and haggling during their confidential meeting. I must stress the importance of nabbing the doctor. Most of the trouble and tribulation over the years can be laid at his feet!"

Her icy blue eyes flash like the fan when she adds, "We will accomplish our mission of bringing these kingdom leaders and their lackies to justice. It won't be easy, nor will our goals be achieved without loss. Remember the Blind Bear's confidence in us...and that he believed only the Autumn Leaves could pull off this raid!"

Sentinel stations along the river scan the territory ceded to the rebel armies after the Battle of Bloody Bridge. All is quiet. This is how the youth soldiers like it. They are excited because their superiors have announced a special televised performance from the count's fortress by the masked dancer troupe that passed through their lines two days ago.

They remember the graceful, almost doll-like girls, and their shimmering dresses, as they passed through the lines. The porcelain masks—mysterious and tantalizing—are especially intriguing, making them wonder what beauty lies hidden underneath.

In keeping with the celebratory spirit and efforts to boost morale, alcoholic beverages and recreational drugs will be provided to rank-and-file soldiers at the front. They also expect Count Thaddeus to announce a new war campaign aimed at taking back lost ground and punishing the rebels and their allies.

Drunken soldiers whose minds are focused on sensuous dancers make mistakes. The greatest is their failure to properly monitor a network of sonar buoys in the river channel. They expect occasional false pings caused by the debris of battle: flotsam of metal and ceramic armor from wrecked military vehicles swept downstream, masses of sunken debris tumbling along the river's bottom—and, of course, bloated corpses.

They log as phantom pings two alarms from widely separated buoys that monitor the entrance of a small harbor where supplies formerly were landed. The rebel toys have since destroyed the docks and crane. Nothing of value to the war effort remains.

The harbor's shallow water is covered by a thick layer of oil, trash and dead fish. Underneath, however, a fleet of submersible troop- and tank-carriers nose into the mud. Invisible and silent, they are part of an assault force waiting to unleash hellfire on the unsuspecting kingdom armies.

"You are in no danger from me."

The youth speaks to the bristling scout snake and Blind Bear with a calming voice, followed by an infectious laugh.

Nodding to Adderlene, he says, "You can deactivate your weapons and rest easy. My ancestors in the Congo were very familiar with yours. Although a bio-mechanical warrior, your genetics derived from the African pit viper clan. The jungle home once shared by humans, serpents and other creatures was wiped from the earth when warlords dared to use nuclear weapons in their struggle for power."

The Bear rests a reassuring paw on Adderlene, but she maintains her rigid vigilance, forked tongue rapidly flicking. The prosthetic sensory and weapons hood expands even further, revealing the nose cones of six small missiles, three on each side. She can unleash the armament individually or in a barrage.

"Who are you?" asks the Bear.

"I am one of the few Mars colony survivors, and I have a story to share."

The teen slowly and carefully rises, holding his hands palm out, while approaching the seated the Blind Bear.

"Your bodyguard would fry me to cinders if you gave the word, sir. But you won't for three reasons. First, you are curious. Second, you seek the truth."

"And the third?" asks Bear.

"You want peace, too. Your life has been full of blood and destruction, but you recall a time when a parentless human child loved you. This is a part of the heritage you have locked away. Living toys and children were not intended to be slaves and masters...nor enemies. The relationship was originally based on mutual love and kindness."

The Blind Bear is dumbfounded. "How do you know these things?"

Burl Sook interrupts, "He is the last member of the Congolese Tutsi people. Several thousand of them sought to escape the curse of drug use and resulting mass suicide by volunteering to settle and terraform Mars. Their thriving colony was wiped out in the invasion's first wave."

"My name is Daniel Mwamba, and the invasion to which he refers is the reason for our visit to your planet," says the youth.

"There is much more at stake here than an ongoing feud between child kingdoms and their former slave toys. The real threat is extinction of all life in our solar system by a cosmic evil that cares nothing about our history or future."

Bear finds it difficult to process the information. So many things have been thrown at him, much of it extraordinary and fanciful. How can he tell truth from lies in this situation?

"I find it hard to believe…"

Daniel Mwamba laughs again, and the other creatures in the control room join.

"Seeing is believing, is it not?" says the youth. "What if we gave you a gift that would allow clearer understanding of our mission and demonstrate why we want your help—and how badly you need ours?"

"What kind of gift?" the Bear wonders out loud.

"Your eyesight," whispers Burl Sook, squeezing the Blind Bear's paw. "We can restore your vision."

Count Thaddeus, self-conscious about craning his neck backwards to look up at the kaiju immobilized in titanium chains and body clamps, tries to reassure himself that Dr. Congesto has complete control of the beast. He's been promised there will be no repeat of the slaughter and destruction at the genetics lab, a failure by the insane scientist that nearly negated the elements of shock and fear crucial to the upcoming military campaign.

The Count, appearing older than his actual age, is still a teenager, but he cultivates the image of a wiser, more experienced human adult. This serves him in good stead when dealing with self-centered, prideful peers—some of whom are psychopathic killers and others criminal hedonists.

The monster seems asleep, great scaled chest rising and falling. Occasionally, a deep rumbling growl declares its reptile brain is active at a low level, despite the tanker-truck pumping a witch's brew of tranquilizing drugs into its bloodstream.

"It's hungry," the Count reminds himself out loud. "The damned thing is always hungry, but the problem is it can't distinguish friend from foe!"

He turns to the doctor, a wizened old man kept alive with mechanical organs, blood transfusions, and toxic chemical injections deadly to normal human beings. Congesto's unsavory reputation includes a penchant for experimenting on himself—replacing natural appendages and sensory organs with biomechanical versions—and rumors about inventing the highly addictive suicide drug responsible for retarding civilization.

"It eats when and where I decide!" the doctor wheezes through a complex face mask sewn to his head with blood-oozing stitches. The Count's spies tell him Congesto barely escaped with his miserable life during the kaiju's last rampage. Three times, he has lost control of the monster.

"No, when I decide!" Count Thaddeus barks.

"Your previous failures with the control system not only cost lives, but you violated the terms of our contract. This monster has been bought and paid for. Our agreement calls for control and transport systems to be successfully tested by a date certain. Today, in fact. But I see your minions still trying to debug technical problems that will endanger the mission and the combined kingdom military forces. If the monster can't be trusted off its leash, it is no use to us!"

Congesto makes a sound like a rat being squashed underfoot.

"Eeeee, all will be ready by midnight! Things will be perfect. These are minor issues, and corrective measures are already implemented, m'Lord."

Stooped and limping, the genetic vivisectionist almost prostrates himself before the looming kaiju, throwing out skinny arms pockmarked by needles and raw from rejected skin graft experimentation.

"It is my most magnificent creation, don't you think?"

The doctor wheezes with pride, seems to actually be hugging himself.

This remains to be seen, the Count thinks. He is tired of arguing with the scientist and turns to depart.

"Sir, just one other thing…if you please?"

The Count wants to curse but instead grinds his teeth and asks, "What new problem haven't you told me about?"

Congesto sidles to the Count's side, like a mongrel dog begging its master for a tidbit of meat. Chemical stink wafts from his garments and body. This close, Thaddeus can see the jagged track marks of sharp scalpel cuts on exposed skin, oozing pustules and inflamed areas of infection. He wants to retch.

"My spectacular creation will not disappoint you," the doctor pledges for the umpteenth time. His breath is rotten, and the Count can see lice wriggling on his sparsely-haired scalp.

"However, to ensure a high energy level and maximum bloodthirstiness, the kaiju needs a good feed before the attack kicks off. Several dozen of your least capable soldiers and toy slaves would be worth sacrificing for assurance of the long-sought-after victory. Hmmm?"

The Count ponders, then snaps his manicured fingers.

"Oh, the monster's meal will be much better than the dross of idiots and traitorous servants. How about a troupe of dancers? I'll have no need of them after the performance. The kaiju can have a buffet of talent and beauty, too. Bon Appetit!"

He strides away, convinced the scientist has outlived his usefulness. When the control system proves reliable and his technicians are trained in operation, the Count has decided Dr. Congesto will have an unfortunate accident. Perhaps the kaiju will eat its creator, too.

In the meantime, the clock is ticking for the counter-attack.

Garden in the Coffin, Coffin in a Cage

Liviu Surugiu
Translation Sebi Simion
Edited by Elise Abram and Jessica West

Thom Clavel found the little box of seeds in one of the walnut desk's drawers. It was about the size of a cigarette case, black with gold inlays. Made in China, surely.

The phone rang as he was studying it.

"Mr. Clavel?" said the same voice he'd heard not fifteen minutes before. "This is Jones from Jones and Philips. Have you reached a decision?"

"Guess so," Thom mumbled, spilling the seeds into his palm and putting the box back. "Would you like a description of the furniture?" He pushed the drawer back into place.

"No need. Your grandmother bought it from us."

So, it was only some poor imitation. He dropped the seeds into his pocket.

"We have the receipt for every armchair and sofa," the voice explained. "We're offering seven thousand."

"Eight," Thom said due to force of habit.

"Done. We'll pick it up in an hour."

The house was large and deserted. The furniture in question consisted of only a couple of armchairs, the desk, and an empty bookcase. With eight thousand dollars—more than he'd expected—he could furnish the kitchen and have some left over for the garden.

Jones arrived earlier than promised. He was joined by two sturdy fellows who quickly swept everything up into a truck. Glad to have the money, Thom got soiled trying to help them. When they were done, he waved at them and dusted himself off at the garden's edge.

Tidying up the house took him almost a week.

When he went into the garden for the first time, he saw a partially unearthed carrot at the far end of it. Weeds had grown on the parcel overcoming the fence, but around the yellow object, they'd gone completely dry.

Yellow?

Huh!

Thomas frowned; its color meant it was no carrot. He circled it once. Maybe it was a parsnip. No, it wasn't that either. Thom sat on a rock, trying to recall whatever he could about horticulture.

That was it—a beetroot!

Nonsense. It couldn't be that either.

The next morning, he ran straight to the garden. A light rain had fallen during the night, and the monstrous vegetable seemed to have gotten so strong that, instead of going back into the earth, it was doing its best to come out. Thom decided he was dealing with a carrot/potato hybrid; he was delighted to dub it a cartato.

He went to Boston for a few days to bring over the rest of his luggage. Shannen had promised she'd follow as soon as she'd gotten her transfer, which was pretty unlikely, considering her job.

Thom saw it from the road. He left the car and went straight into the garden where his enthusiasm was quickly choked out.

The hybrid had assumed the shape of a hand. Its long fingers dipped into the earth as if it were trying to bury something.

He wasted half an hour on the phone with people from various greenhouses and botanical gardens. In the end, he calmed down. This was normal. A caretaker from Nevada had a whole crop of similar peculiarities, all of them human-shaped, and an old lady in Texas had been keeping a tomato with the face of an Indian in her fridge for the past three months, waiting for someone from *Guinness*.

In the afternoon, he moved the cartato into a huge pot—more like a trough made from a barrel he'd cut in half. It looked too good to be left alone, and he was so very bored. Shannen wouldn't visit until the weekend, at the earliest.

He put down his luggage, had a bite to eat, and went into town. When he turned the corner, a neighbor stopped to tell him he'd miraculously gotten rid of his Colorado potato beetles—he'd seen them flying toward the lake.

The following day, he considered replanting the cartato into Grandma's spare coffin, since it had outgrown the barrel. Cautious by nature, Grandma had ordered an extra one in case she got fatter before she died.

Thom dragged the funeral piece from the shed into the living room and then, with a contraption worthy of the ancient Egyptians, lifted it onto the table.

As dusk fell, he thought about planting two poisonous colchicums next to the cartato. At first, they seemed to be doing well, but they withered within two days.

He no longer watered the oddity in the coffin—he'd grown quite bored of it—so when he came home from work, he wasn't particularly surprised to see it had extended its leaves over the table, reaching for a glass of water. This sparked a phytotechnological instinct in him, prompting him to plant two very spiky cacti in the coffin before he went to bed.

In the morning, he found only two holes in the dried soil, and a few spikes stuck into the edge of the coffin instead of the cacti, as if someone had desperately tried to climb up from burial there. He celebrated the cartato's victory by pouring a bucket of water on it.

Afterward, he conceded that he should also probably soothe his throat as well—Shannen's absence had somehow made him thirstier than usual.

"Mr. Cartato," he said, sitting next to the coffin and raising a glass. "I am a vegetable, good sir. That is our common trait!"

He spilled a few drops of whiskey over the deathly black earth.

They celebrated Shannen's arrival properly. His fiancé seemed thrilled with their new home, but she went pale when she saw the coffin in the living room.

Thom smiled as he explained that it was nothing more than a passing hobby. He actually mumbled that it had been his grandmother's dying wish, but he would change everything the following day, and then he went out to buy what was on his list.

When he came back, he found Shannen lying on the kitchen floor. Thom called an ambulance, but first, he opened the windows because the steam from the boiling pot had filled the room.

Shannen had green spots all over her face, and tiny, pus-filled sores covered her arms. She came to for a minute at the hospital, enough to tell him, albeit not coherently, what had happened, how she was about to make soup, and since he hadn't shown up with the carrots...

Thom barged into the house blinded with anger, clutching the ax from the shed with both hands. He was at the coffin in two strides and split the carrot—for that's what he called it now: just a carrot. He struck it again, feeling as if the blade was cutting through sinew and bone. He filled the coffin with the slices and cubes which, as they were being halved, grew dark orange, almost red.

He had nightmares that night and went to work early, avoiding the living room. They hadn't allowed him to sit with Shannen for a long while in the hospital. The allergy, intoxication, or whatever the hell she had, would not subside.

Thom came home just as angry, if not more so, knowing he had no one on which to take out his vengeance.

He opened the living room door, and a small cry escaped from his lips. The coffin on the table was full of small, new, orange hands. Each of them had their fingertips stuck in the dirt, with enough space between the buried fingers to allow Thom a glimpse of what they held in their five-barred cages. Each of them held a seal, a stamp, a mark.

He plucked one off and stuck it to the wall. The fresh soil left a dirty mark on the white paint in the shape of small, circular letters that read "Stanford University." He took another. This one read "Louisiana State Penitentiary." Then "Oxford Artificial Intelligence," "Los Angeles City Hall," "Ohio Army National Guard," "Banks & Credit Union Mortgage Lenders…"

There were also seals from the time of Babylon, hieroglyphs of Sanherib of Nimrud, Phoenician stamps, Pilate's name…

Tens of hundreds of stamps!

Sculpted into potatoes.

He recalled his college years, when he'd forged his doctor's stamp on a note to justify his many periods of absence.

Thom started to think.

It would have been easy for some capable person to have inserted these options directly into the plants' genetic code, and then all they had to do was turn them into wooden stamps, no whittling required.

Thom decided that things had taken an interesting turn, something that might turn him a tidy profit. And why not? He could even have some fun with it.

He went outside and dug around in his neighbor's manure pile for almost two hours, stopping only when his jar was full of mole crickets. Thom went to the edge of the coffin and let them go inside. The tiny battleships went immediately under.

Thom Clavel sat in his armchair for hours. He ran to the kitchen and came back with a bowl of soup, but he spat it out after the first mouthful, wondering if Shannen had managed to put a *piece* of that thing inside the pot.

He fell asleep in the armchair, waking up a few times before dawn. Each time he looked, but nothing was going on inside the coffin. The light from the lamp shone over the arm-filled earth, like the sunset on Easter Island.

Thom went to the hospital early in the morning, but they didn't even let him in. They'd moved Shannen to the contagious ward. She was still unconscious.

On his way home, he stopped by Home Depot and a pet shop.

When he went back into the living room, his face was glowing. It didn't take long for him to set the up the net. Fifteen minutes later, he was sure he was the first person ever to put a coffin inside a cage. But that wasn't all—in an ongoing boost of imagination, Thom pulled a spotted rabbit out of a bag and forced it into the coffin.

He went for a walk. When he came back from the bar down the street about an hour later, the rabbit was dead.

The doorbell rang, snatching him away from his doubts. When he opened the door, a man in a black suit walked past him and looked carefully around. He motioned to two other men behind him to come in. The two sturdy fellows, dressed in green overalls with tags on the bibs that read "Jones & Phillips" began to search the house as if they'd had search warrants.

"I found them, boss!" one of them cried from the living room.

The other men rushed over.

"I'll be damned!" Jones said. "Come on! We'll take them *and* the coffin!"

Thom wound up on the floor when he tried to stop them.

The men went past Thom. One of their heavy boots stomped his hand, and he sat up with a cry of pain.

He moved his shattered fingers to his blood-crusted lips. Then, he slowly stood to look out the window, trying not to sway, and he touched the blinds.

Jones had tripped out in the yard. All three men had fallen. The coffin had flipped over, covering their legs in dirt.

They didn't scream.

Thom slowly locked the door, crawled back to the window, and saw with horror and not a little bit of satisfaction, the sickly yellow-orange fluid as it climbed up the paralyzed bodies of the three men.

Every living thing the foul juice touched died. Thom reflected how it was a good thing it wasn't the other way around.

There was a knock at the door.

"Who are you?" Tom asked, looking through the peephole.

A thin man covered in dirt swayed in front of him, just beyond the *very* frail, wooden door. His clothes were torn, and it seemed as if his brittle hair was slowly falling out.

"Who are you?" Thom asked again, noticing the steam rising from a hole behind the stranger. "What do you want?" he asked, growing increasingly scared.

The hole was close to where the orange substance had spilled from the coffin.

"Y...ear?" the hideous thing slurred.

Thom could barely contain his fear.

"Ye...ar?" it said again.

It wasn't a mobster—it was just some guy in rotten clothes.

He gave no answer, but he crawled to the kitchen to look for an ax.

The thing outside left, stumbling through the garden at a slower and slower pace, reminding Thom of a toy in need of a key spin. He stared at the thing, desperately searching for something, a certain root, a certain mark.

He lost track of time.

Night fell.

The hospital called to tell him that Shannen had died. It didn't matter anymore because the unearthed man from the garden had found *it*—whatever it was he'd been looking for. It was too dark for Thom to see him clearly anymore, but he did hear the thing, chanting as it went through the gate and into the road: "And one of the angels had the seal of death, while the other had the seal of life…And one of the angels had the seal of death, while the other had the seal of life…And one of the…"

Thom took a deep breath—it felt like a lifeline being dangled in front of him like a carrot before being choking to death—then went to the back door. He had to bring Shannen home. He had to bring her to the garden.

One More Night
Lara Frater

<u>Check List and Inventory</u>
Dead roommate moved to the vestibule— To do
Doors and chain locked— Check
Every single empty container filled with water— Check
Gas, water, and electricity— still working for now
Internet and phone— Sporadic

<u>Amount of Food</u>
Unknown amount of perishables in the fridge, working on that first
7 boxes of spaghetti
10 cans of tomato paste (WTF Donnie)
2 cans of corn
3 cans of lima beans
½ Jar peanut butter
4 cans of peas
8 cases of ramen (Thanks CostKing!)

<u>Amount of booze</u>
12 bottles of beer
1 bottle of vodka

1 bottle of tequila
Half bottle of rum
1 and a ½ bottles of red wine

A Long December by Counting Crows on Repeat— Trying to turn it off

"Hi, Mom, Dad. It's Shawn again. I hope you're okay. Please call me as soon as possible. I'm worried."

I end the call. My parents always answer but haven't in the last three days.

My neighbor Ben has always been a Counting Crows fan. On the day the movers came with my stuff, *Mr. Jones* played at top volume. Ben is... was an okay guy, but despite claiming to be the Crows' number one fan, he tended to play their three biggest songs the most and never anything recent. And I checked. *Counting Crows* still makes albums. Well, probably not now.

I can't get into Ben's apartment next door even though we share an enclosed courtyard and I'm pretty sure I can jiggle his window open. Every time I try, Ben comes to the window. His skin has faded to chalk and when he opens his mouth, what looks like congealed grease comes out.

I haven't tried again.

Even though we're in our 20's, and Ben is in his late 40's, when Ben had parties he invited us and when we had parties we invited him. He wasn't a horrible party guest, and his parties were good for a few hours of free booze.

Apparently, he sold insurance.

Now, *A Long December* plays on repeat from dead Ben's apartment. And it has been playing for the last three days while the world died. If I have to hear about the dreads and wonders of LA and life for any longer, I might become a zombie too.

He didn't have an Alexa. Believe me, I know. The first night, I screamed, "Alexa!" until I was hoarse, hoping it would shut the music off. Either it didn't hear me or he didn't have one. I tended to tune out Ben when he spoke. He talked a lot about his job, how many times he'd seen the Crows in the late 90's, and how his ex-wife is a bitch.

Everyone is dead. I mean, I don't know how it is worldwide. Everyone I knew had the flu and I think they're dead, but some of them have become zombies. My roommate died and stayed dead, but Ben didn't. He got bit by his undead girlfriend. At least that's what I think happened.

Now both of them are undead creatures in his apartment. This means that *A Long December* will continue playing as long as there is electricity.

It isn't like I hate the band, but hearing about days in canyons and nights in Hollywood for seventy-two hours can get tedious. Not tedious—maddening.

Now I know the entire song. Even when I'm in my room with the door closed and have music playing out of my phone, I still hear it.

However, most of the time I'm in the kitchen, sorting through the food, deciding how long I have before I need to go out and forage. I hear it loudest in the kitchen.

The trains stopped running yesterday. Last night, there was a derailment in Huntington and the entire system shut down.

Yesterday, I heard shots and that's the last I heard of human sounds except for Adam Duritz.

So here I am. Enough food for a few weeks and a long December ahead of me, even though it's May. No one picks up at 911. I try everyone I know dozens of times.

No response. I call and text every number on my list. Even my doctor and dentist. No response.

My roommate, Donnie, didn't keep a lot of food in the house. He's skinny and I hate him. Not because of his body size, not because when we have parties and invite girls, they flock to him and avoid me. I hate him because all he is… was, is a giant fucking moocher.

We met in our dorms in college and after school decided to be roommates. At the time, we both worked full time, then he lost his job a few months later. He always said he was looking. It didn't matter now. Two days ago, Donnie got the flu and by evening, he was dead. In the morning, I wrapped his dead body in luxurious silk sheets. Expensive sheets he bought after he claimed poverty.

A Long December ends then starts up again. There are exactly three seconds between the end and the beginning where I have blissful silence. I know I need electricity, but part of me wants it to go out so the music stops.

Today I have to remove the roommate. Drag his bloated, stinky, slimy corpse down the stairs and through the hallway and maybe outside.

I debate putting him in the courtyard but I remember the Christmas tree.

When we first moved in, Donnie got a live tree. When it was time to dispose of it, Donnie thought it would be a great idea to put it in the courtyard until tree recycling day. I went along with it, probably because I was drunk. We tried each window to the courtyard with disastrous results by tracking pine needles and branches all over. We finally dragged the thing back to the corner of the living room. Afterwards, anytime I did remember to clean, I would find pine needles.

I make the executive decision to take him outside.

Which carries its own risk. Outside means zombies.

I don't do this all at once. I'm not in shape to drag a body. First, I take him to the door, still wrapped in sheets. When I'm done, I take a breath and go to the kitchen for a glass of water from the tap, knowing not to waste the already bottled water. Then I wash it down with a vodka chaser.

My next step is to drag him into the hallway to the top of the stairs. His bloat makes him heavier.

I stare at the double doors at the bottom of the stairs. One door is glass and leads to a vestibule. The wooden door in the vestibule leads to the outside.

And since I don't have the strength, I drop Donnie at the top of the stairs and let him slide down.

Which he did spectacularly.

The sheets make him slippery and he slides right down and hits the door hard. I hear a crack but it isn't the door.

"Jeez, sorry Donnie."

But I don't follow him to the bottom. Instead, I debate if I should leave him and finish tomorrow.

I turn around and walk the small hallway between my apartment and Ben's. I knock on the door.

I hear my dead neighbor rushing. He smacks against the door hard. I hear moans.

"Serves you right."

I go back to the top of the stairs and sit on the top step. Falling down the stairs has caused some of the sheets to unravel, revealing Donnie's decaying bloated arm. Even though Donnie has only been in the hallway for a few minutes, he already stinks up the place. I have to get him out.

I head downstairs to his body and wish I'm wearing a bandana around my face.

I have to figure out how to do this.

Should I open the front door and make sure things are all clear? Or should I just open the door and toss him out?

I guess the first thing I should do is move him between the inner and outer doors. I open the inner door and drag Donnie by the arm into the vestibule.

I get to the outer door but don't open it. Instead, I look out the peephole and see the street. I wait a moment, but no zombies, people, or cars come by.

I look around the vestibule. Mail hasn't been picked up. I spy a package from Amazon for Ben, so I nab it and put it to the side. Ben won't be using it and it might be useful.

"Okay, Donnie. We have to do this. Can't have you stinking up the place."

Donnie, under his sheet, says nothing.

I place my hand on the door and open it.

No zombies in my vision. I grab Donnie by the shoulders and begin pulling him out.

I hear a moan seconds later. I look up. A zombie is almost right on top of me. She came from the store next door, which was out of my vision.

The zombie is the woman who owns the jewelry store below our apartment who complains about everything. Every sound we make. The worst was when a pipe broke under our bathtub, leaked into her store, and she acted like we did it on purpose. Like Donnie and I were jumping up and down in our bathtub.

And now she is about to eat me, or whatever zombies do.

Luckily, I have Donnie between us and I use him as a meat shield. When she goes in for a bite, I use all my strength to lift Donnie up so she bites him instead. She sinks her teeth into Donnie's chest. I thank whatever is up there she gets her teeth stuck in the sheet.

I drop Donnie, who pulls the shopkeeper down with him. I make a mad dash for the door. I see more zombies coming in my direction, but for just a moment I glance over the street. No sign of people, and abandoned cars sit in the street. I go in and slam the door hard and lock it. I lock the vestibule door too. I grab Ben's package, climb up the stairs in the middle of the song, and, even though I'm out of breath, I don't stop until I'm inside my apartment.

I slam this door too, and put all the locks on, including the chain.

I open the box from Amazon, rip it open with gusto, and find it filled with underwear and socks.

Fuck you, Ben.

The song ends. I get three seconds of peace.

I go to my room and close the door. I put a pillow over my head. I can still hear the song, but it's faint. The whole situation leaves me overwhelmed both physically and mentally. I need rest.

I look at my iPhone. No messages, no texts. My last text from yesterday was my best friend asking me to head north with him. I said yes. And that was the last I heard from him.

Either he never got my text or he's dead. I call him again and get voicemail.

I wonder if Donnie would smell and if I should risk moving him further into the street. Instead, I pull the blanket over my head and close my eyes.

I wake to complete darkness. I notice right away the song isn't playing.

I look at my phone. It's no longer charging.

All I can hear are their moans outside my window. Did it seem like more now or is it just because of the quiet?

I turn on the lamp.

No more power.

I stumble to the bathroom in an inky blackness that scares me.

I feel for the tap and come in contact with it. I turn it, hear a spurt, and then nothing. No water.

I stand there in the dark in my bathroom.

And know there will be no more nights in Hollywood.

The Courier

Daniel Arthur Smith

The Courier approached from the shadows, wading shin deep through the woolen mist blanketing the alley, the hard soles of his shoes slapping against the shallow-puddled cobblestone so that the echo of his steps came before him. *Schlapp, schlapp, schlapp.*

A single, grime coated sliver of LED beside the old metal door emitted a dull light that bathed the aged brickwork at the end of the narrow alley in a ball of sepia monochrome, a contrast to the vibrant shades of neon illuminating the outer avenue.

The Courier stopped at the edge of the light, the beads of condensation covering his black fedora and the shoulders of his long coat sparkling orange in the reflection of the LED, his face hidden behind thick, fish eyed goggles and a respirator, and in his right hand he held a thick, boxy, black briefcase. Even with freshly charged cartridges on either side of his breathing mask, the stench he had stirred with each step seeped through, an unsavory stew of chemical remnants accumulated from the hundreds of environmental control units that peppered the towers above.

The squat man glanced back over his shining shoulder and listened to the hum of the avenue behind him by chance he'd been followed. Satisfied, he turned his attention back toward the door, an undisturbed back ally entrance, a throwback to history, untouched, sterile, exactly the type of back door he preferred. Rarely did he make a delivery through the front door if he could help it.

The Courier stepped up to the old, corroded metal door, his bulbous head and thick goggles shifting slightly left to right, then up and down, as he inspected it. The door was indeed ancient—no doubt part of the original structure the towers of the new city above were built upon—but the symbol stenciled in white over the bubbled rust high in the top center was unmistakable: the Korean *jamo* specifically created for the syndicate. This was the right place.

The Courier raised a plump, black-gloved left hand and knocked three times.

Thunk, thunk, thunk.

With a snap, the small panel in the speakeasy slot below the symbol slid to the side.

At just above four feet, the top of the Courier's fedora was beneath the little window.

"Who's there?" a voice blurted in common.

From behind his mask, the Courier responded, "I have an appointment."

"I can't see you."

The squat man took a step back. The reflective glint of two eyes peeped down through the narrow rectangle in the door.

A palm sized console came to life below the dulled LED. On the grime yellowed screen was an image of the short, stocky, square-shouldered Courier.

"What do you want?" asked the voice behind the door.

"I have an appointment," repeated the Courier.

A green beam of laser light shot out from the console and toward the Courier's feet, rapidly spreading left and right to form a flat fan of light that slowly rose to scan the Courier toe to head. When the fan reached the top of the Courier's fedora, it disappeared; and the small screen flashed bright then held a still image of the man.

"One minute," the voice said.

The little window slapped shut.

The Courier waited, the shining beads on his fedora and wide shoulders gathering into trickling streams from the falling chemical mist, the stank continuing to seep into his mask. A moment passed. Then, without announcement, three loud clacks came from within the door. It swung inward to reveal a small dark hallway and three men—a rotund, baby-faced man at the door and two thin men standing a few feet behind him—all in matching dark suits, white shirts, and thin black ties. The baby-faced doorman gave the Courier another once over. "Okay," he said then stepped to the side and, with a nod, waved him in.

The Courier accepted the invitation and passed through the threshold. Behind him, the door shut with a thud. Three clacks followed. The closest of the two suited men was easily over two meters tall, well above the height of the Courier, and, most noticeably, had glowing, blue lit eyes. The Koreans owned the restricted ocular tech and most all of the syndicate leaders and lieutenants had the lace implant reserved for the Burrough and those traveling off-world.

The tall, blue-eyed man stepped forward, so close that the Courier, his pupils large and fish-eyed in the wide lenses of his thick goggles, had to tilt his head back to peer up at him. Again, the Courier said, "I have an appointment."

The shorter of the two suited men tapped the taller man's shoulder. The tall, blue-eyed man leaned to the side, and the shorter man whispered into his ear. The tall man straightened and nodded in agreement to the whisper. "Okay," he said, then moved to the side so the shorter man could step forward. The shorter man reached into his suit jacket, removed a thin steel wand, then, in a single rapid motion, waved it up and down on either side of the man.

Satisfied the Courier was unarmed, the short man nodded back to the tall one as he returned to his place behind him.

"You'll check to see if someone is following?" asked the Courier.

"Did someone follow you?" asked the tall man.

"It's possible," said the Courier.

The tall man nodded to the rotund man at the door and the Courier heard the speakeasy window slap open again then shut. The tall man then lowered his blue-eyed gaze from the door down to the big black case in the Courier's hand. He mouthed something soft and inaudible as he shifted his focus to the squat man's respirator masked face.

The Courier determined the blue-eyed man was speaking to someone not in the small room through a com, most likely a chin-chip, another shared Bureau tech. The Courier read his lips.

The tall man's blue eyes rested back down on the case as he softly described it. After a pause, the tall man nodded in response to whatever voice was in his head. "Okay," he said aloud. "Come this way." Then he gestured for his shorter colleague to lead the way.

The Courier followed the short, black suited man out of the hallway into a storage room; the tall man fell in behind. They walked down an aisle of ceiling high racks holding uniformed containers to either side. At the end of the aisle, they turned and walked along the wall past three more identical storage aisles before turning into the dishwashing area of a large kitchen.

The Courier, meticulous to detail, counted four dishwashers: three men and one woman, clad in white, their hair tucked into round white pill caps. One scrubbed a large steel wok, the woman, and another manned the dishwashing machine. The fourth moved stacked plates to a window. The four worked without notice of the three.

From the dishwashing station, the three marched into a large prep area where the Courier counted eight white uniformed men and women manning stations aside huge steel tables as they chopped vegetables and huge protein cakes with cleavers while others manned rows of sizzling woks and tall boiling pots along the stoves that lined the back and far side wall. At the opposite end of a long table, a delivery man in a brown uniform stood with a box of produce as one of the kitchen workers sorted through the contents. None even turned to glance at the Courier and his escorts.

The three approached the double doors to the dining room and stopped at the end of a long steel counter where an assembly line of kitchen workers on one side each added components to big bowls and plates: hills of uniform spun noodles topped with sauteed vegetables and proteins then finally covered in thick bronze sauces or thin golden broths. Upon completion, each plate was slid forward to be picked up by a river of black-uniformed waiters. The Courier scowled beneath his mask due to his discomfort with the variant number of waitstaff as they entered through the doors at the far end of the counter with trays in hand, loaded them with the ready to serve plates, then exited to the front of where the three were standing. Like the dishwashers and cooks, the servers paid no mind to the three, prompting the short man leading the three to continue to wait lest he be run down as two servers with huge trays barreled past them and through a set of double doors. When a break in the flow of servers came, the short man reached up to push the doors open for the three. A bloody butcher knife flew in front of the Courier's face and planted itself into the wall. The Courier spun his head in time to watch another knife fly from the hand of the produce delivery man, and the worker beside him fell onto the grill, a fist sized patch of red soaking his chest. The blue-eyed escort shoved the Courier forward into the arms of the shorter man, then sprung up onto the long steel table. As he leapt toward the assailant, the short man lunged backward through the server doors with his arms wrapped around the Courier and into the dark faux wood paneled restaurant bar. The short escort then swung the Courier to the front of him and pushed his ward along the side of the restaurant. The Courier scanned the path in front of him as his feet shuffled into each other. He scanned each of the faces of the age modded perpetually young-looking patrons, well dressed in suits and evening dresses, dining unaware from their plates with steel chopsticks. Though his feet were tripping up each other, the Courier counted thirty-three. From the dark restaurant, they shuffled into the casino, a high-ceilinged hall full of large, bright gambling machines, with more patrons parked in front of them, tapping at large blueberries, large red cherries, and aubergine eggplants as the images rained down the two-meter-high, color filled, flashing screens. The Courier's wide eyes darted side to side, counting the gamblers in twos, threes, and fours, as the short man continued to speed him through the maze of bright blinking fruit machines, turning right down a long curving aisle, then left through another, right into another.

They came to fork in the maze, the left path blocked by a man in a yellow worker's jumpsuit, toolbox in hand. They veered right not to lose momentum to find a pink haired cocktail waitress running toward them.

The two backtracked and spun toward the left fork. The man in the yellow jumpsuit was on one knee, his hand pulling a blaster from his toolbox. The short escort pulled his *sabre*, a handheld weapon that could shoot an energized bolt or project an energized blade, and raised it toward the worker. From behind them, two blasts of energy raced past the escort's face, exploding the two-meter screen of the fruit machine at the fork. It was another assassin in yellow running up the aisle from behind. The escort shot blindly toward the kneeling worker as he spun to target the approaching third assassin.

The Courier turned back toward the right aisle. The running woman dove forward into a cartwheel, her bright pink, shoulder length hair wildly fanning out. The short escort had ignited his blade to deflect the energy blasts the charging assassin shot toward him while at the same time he rapidly kicked his right foot into the face of the kneeling assailant.

The woman launched from her cartwheel into a somersault, pulled two curved blades from beneath her short skirt and corrected to a dive toward the Courier. The Courier swung up his gloved left hand, palm out toward the woman, his goggles glowed tangerine, and a translucent tangerine tinted bubble formed around him. The woman struck the bubble full force, blades first then bounced off, and slammed full body into a tall game screen, sending a spiderweb of cracks across it from the impact. The Courier shifted his gloved hand towards her, his tangerine glowing goggles shifting to bright lemon yellow. The pink haired woman recovered to a crouching pose, ready to spring froward, still gripping a curved blade in each hand. But rather than launch her svelte self, she froze, mesmerized by the Courier's bright glowing goggles. Her shoulders, arms, and fingers went limp. The blades slipped from her hands onto the floor beside her. A drop of blood trickled from her nose then another from the inner corner of her eye.

The blasting behind the Courier reached crescendo then an energized bolt struck the woman's head, scattering pink hair, skull fragments, and brain matter into the aisle.

Only the carnival chimes of the fruit machines remained.

The bubble surrounding the Courier and the light in his goggles quickly faded as he turned back around to find his two escorts standing side by side, the yellow jumpsuit wearing assassins dead on the ground behind them, and the barrel of his blue-eyed escort's weapon pointed to where the woman had been.

Without hesitation, the escorts each grabbed one of the Courier's arms and hustled him forward.

The blue-eyed man rattled silent orders through his com as he shoved patrons aside.

The three emerged from the maze of bright screened fruit machines into the table section of the casino. Players circled table after table, throwing dice, throwing tiles, throwing gold and red and silver colored casino chips onto grids of numbered squares as wheels spun. The Courier quantified the number of people at each table, taking note of their actions and behavior.

A man in a beige suit rounded a table in front of them, blocking their way forward. He reached into his jacket and pulled a pistol. The blue-eyed escort blasted a fist sized hole through the would be assassins chest. Screams and shouts shot out from the surrounding crowd but the escorts did not stop.

They turned from the tables into a high walled hallway. Patrons filed in and out of the tiled tunnels to the restrooms to the right, while to the left, a bay of three elevator doors held a half dozen more men in the same black suit uniforms as the Courier's escorts. They stood on alert in front of them.

Without a word, the guard in the middle of the group stepped forward to make room for the three.

The short man leading the three approached the door, stopped inches in front of it, and leaned toward a tiny electric eye. A laser shot into the escort's retina. Two energized blasts erupted from the other end of the hallway, the first glowing bolt flew past the escort, the second exploded his head.

The Courier scanned the end of the crowded hall, his view partially blocked by the black suited syndicate soldiers surrounding him. The soldiers were blasting their weapons toward a group of charging assassins, some in yellow jumpsuits, some dressed as patrons, all charging forward.

Another energized bolt slipped past the Courier's protectors, barely missing his right arm. His goggles again glowed tangerine as his black gloved hand flew up toward the assailants.

The black suited soldier in front of the Courier fell from the opposing fire. He stepped over him, a barrage of bright red energized bolts ricocheting from the surface of his protective bubble. The blue-eyed escort and a few others deflected blasts with long, ignited *sabre* blades while others were blasting, and the assailants did the same, so that the five meter distance between the two groups was a maelstrom of flying light. The Courier's goggles brightened to a lemon yellow. The group of assailants stopped blasting and defending. Three last blasts from the suited syndicate soldiers landed their targets, causing a patron dressed assailant and a yellow jumpsuit to drop.

Confused, their weapons still drawn, the syndicate soldiers stopped blasting. Blood trickled from the noses and eyes of the assailants. The light of the Courier's goggles intensified. The syndicate soldiers shielded their eyes from the blinding bright light.

The hallway flashed lightening white as two thick arcs lashed out from the Courier's goggles toward the assailants, vaporizing them where they stood.

Fear flooded the face of the blue-eyed escort as he mouthed something into the com. But then he stepped to the small electric eye beside the elevator and leaned into it. The laser shot out again, this time into the blue eye of the Courier's escort. The elevator's panel doors slid open.

Brow furrowed, the blue-eyed escort peered deeply at the Courier. The piercing gaze was brief, but thorough and telling—the escort was reassessing the unassuming courier. The tangerine tinted bubble was gone and wide fish eyes filled the clear goggles. Blue-eyes appeared undecided in his analysis but there was no time for hesitation. He gestured the Courier into the cubed lift and signaled another suited foot soldier to join them. The doors slid shut with one escort to either side of the Courier. To the front of the blue-eyed man, where a number pad would be, was a small square of black glass. Blue-eyes placed the tip of his index finger against the pane and again spoke inaudibly. With the faintest sensation of motion, the elevator rose. Pressure slowly built at their feet as the elevator accelerated upward to the heights of the ziggurat tower. Minutes passed before deceleration. As the elevator carriage came to a gentle rest, the squat courier found his belly spinning and stumbled into the new escort. The escort steadied him in time for the doors to slide open to a large, brightly lit, wood paneled office suite with a wall of glass overlooking the cityscape of the meg poking through a sleeping purple-grey cloud. A large CCTV monitor filled the left side wall, split into a grid of smaller screens, detailing areas of the casino floor, some showing replays of the incidents below, and on the right wall was an inlaid cabinet with a row of six bonsai trees behind glass. In the far right corner of the room, near the windowed wall, was a huge wooden desk with two tall chairs in front of it and seated opposite, another young looking man with the same cerulean blue ocular implant and dark suit as the tall escort, but with a fuchsia, open collared shirt.

The seated man reclined in a tall backed, black leather cushioned chair. In one hand, he swirled the remnants of a caramel-colored spirit around the bottom of a rock glass; with the other, he finger-tapped at a screen embedded into the top of his desk. The small screen on his desk went dark as he peered up at the three. The two escorts gave the seated man a deep bow then the blue-eyed escort said, "Your appointment, Mister Lee." Lee nodded in response, downed the remains of his drink, then stood.

"Please," Lee said, gesturing to the two leather chairs on the opposite side of his desk. "Have a seat." Then he turned his back to the three and walked over to a shelf of three caramel spirit filled decanters on the side wall beneath the glass cabinet display.

Without a word, the Courier separated himself from his two taller escorts and went to the desk. He lifted the large case as he sat, placed it on his lap, and folded his gloved hands over the top handle.

While his host opened a decanter, the Courier inspected the room, his eyes filling the wide lensed goggles.

"Yes," Lee said without turning his head. "The walls, the desk, real wood." The Courier did not respond. Lee poured two fingers of spirit from the decanter into his glass then the same in a second for his guest. "From the Farm Plane," he continued, "but real all the same." He spun around, two glasses in hand. "The leather too. Real."

Lee walked to the side of the desk, set down the drink he poured for the Courier in front of him, then returned to his own high backed chair. He reclined back as he sat, relaxed, glass in hand, then gazed at the Courier. "You're still wearing your respirator," he said, and inhaled a long breath into his nostrils then slowly exhaled. "The air is sweet in here."

The Courier turned his head back to the right then back to his host.

"Right," said Lee. He placed his thumb to the edge of his desk and a panel beside the wall length CCTV monitor subtly clicked ajar. He then nodded at the two escorts. The two men bowed deeply, then exited through a hidden door.

After the escorts left, Lee raised his brow and shrugged at the Courier.

The squat Courier first removed the fedora from his large head and placed it on the desk. His host winced, but not at the Courier's oversized wingnut ears; it was the two thick, red, angular scars that ran from beneath the straps of his goggles and mask from his right eye and his right ear, up the side of the Courier's bulbous bald brown scalp where they joined near the center, then continued back as a singular jagged red river of swollen flesh, as if the skin had been ripped from his skull then haphazardly patched together. In a time when nanites could heal most anything, it was curious to find such a scar, much less one allowed to heal so crudely.

The Courier removed his goggles to reveal two large bugged out eyes ready to pop free from his face, then finally the respirator mask. The scar above the Courier's right eye ran down through the brow, over lids of his eye, and down to the center of his cheek. From his inside pocket, the Courier pulled out a set of wired spectacles, the glass almost a finger thick, and with the one hand, awkwardly placed them on his face. When the Courier was through, he turned his attention back to his host, his big eyes filling the lenses of his spectacles as they had the goggles.

Lee sipped from the glass in his hand then said, "It's true then. I mean it's been a while since I've needed someone of your caliber."

"What is true?" asked the Courier.

"Still no age mods." The man raised his index finger from his glass and with a slight wag and a pensive half wink added. "The nanites effect your defense tech."

"It's true."

"Hmm," Lee said reminiscing. "Even with all of our technology, some things never change. I assure you I'm much older than you."

The Courier nodded with disinterest.

"Now that we can talk face to face, I am compelled to introduce myself. My name is Bom Lee."

"Mister Lee," the Courier responded.

Confident the Courier would not offer his own name, Lee continued. "Did you have any issues? Apart from the floor I mean."

"No."

Lee nodded, "Well. I assure you all's well now. This office, this floor, is the safest stronghold in the Meg." He drew another drink from his glass. "I suggest you try the whiskey." He held his own his own glass up toward the windowed wall, tilting it to the side so that a thin amber film lined the interior. "Look at the legs, almost syrup and smooth as silk. It was aged in real oak casks, and you can taste the oak."

"After."

Recognizing small talk was lost on the professional, Lee's face lost expression. "May I see it then?" he asked.

The Courier stood, raising the case with his right hand and placing it on the desk before Lee. Lee took note of the thick chained cuff attaching the case to the Courier's wrist along with the thick red cable coiled around it that terminated in one end into the case and the other into the flesh of the Courier's wrist.

"The code please," said the Courier.

"Of course, I certainly wouldn't want you to detonate."

The Courier's face remained blasé.

Offput by the lack of enthusiasm, Lee rattled off the line of poetry necessary to receive the case. "The Crane flew alone, then there were—"

"No," said the Courier. "Slowly and articulate. The code is recognized by intonations of your voice and the space between them."

"Of course," Lee said, mildly amused. "How could I forget." Then slowly and purposely, he recited the line again. "The Crane flew alone, then there were two, eight, nine, and three."

From the case and cuff came a series of clicks and clacks.

The wide cuff fell free from the Courier's wrist, leaving only the thick red cable affixed to the conduit in the his forearm. The squat man rubbed his wrist where the cuff had been then, with a twist, unplugged the cable from the jack in his arm.

But the case remained closed.

"That gives you the case," said the Courier. "You'll use the second code to open it."

"What if I wished to open it now? While you're still here."

"If that is your wish, continue."

Lee cleared his throat then sung three notes of a melody—"La dee da."

Nothing happened.

"Again," said the Courier. "A little louder."

Lee took another swig of his whiskey then sang the melody again, louder, "La dee da."

In immediate response, an electric chime mimicking Lee's song sounded from within the case and at the end of the last note, the top flap of the box popped open. Lee gazed at the Courier. A golden light leaked out from within the box, casting a soft glow onto the Courier's round face.

The squat man nodded and when Lee nodded back, he flipped the top flap up so that the full side panel of the case unfolded onto the desk to reveal a transparent container, a light from within the top brilliantly illuminating a foot high bonsai tree, its ornate weeping branches lush with foliage, and dangling from the delicate branches, small translucent red lantern flowers.

Lee bit into his lower lip as he lost himself in the tree. "It's beautiful," he said.

"I was initially instructed to transport a woman from the pick-up point but was given this case instead. Another bonsai for your collection?"

Lee's head fell to the side as he inspected each branch and blossom. "It's so much more than that."

"Regardless, human or tree, the fee is the same."

"As it should be," said Lee. He reached across the desk and placed his thumb over a small tab of metal at the base of the case. A holographic bust of a young woman appeared around and above the small bonsai. "One of our senior scientists, the esteemed Doctor Kim Yoo, was killed in an um…unfortunate off-world accident. Fortunately, along with DNA, the Lacemaker maintains an active backup of every laced individual's conscience at the Lions Meadow. The tree in this case holds Doctor Yoo's DNA and most importantly, her knowledge."

"So, this tree is her?" asked the Courier.

"The woman you were to transport. In a manner of speaking. Yes."

"But why doesn't she speak? I've seen similar trees in family shrines, but they spoke with the personality of the…of the donor."

"And that's where this tree is different," said Lee. "The personality of the common memorial tree is an AI enhancement of the individual it's built from. With this tree, rather than artificially enhance the personality, it is instead suppressed, so that only aspects of her remain, exceptional aspects of an exceptional mind, bound on the molecular level in this little, priceless, one-of-a-kind tree."

"That valuable?"

"If it wasn't I'd have transported her with an armored mil group rather than have utilized your services." Lee smiled then tapped his desktop to ignite the embedded console. He drummed the fingers of his left hand across the small screen then gestured the whiskey glass toward the row of bonsais displayed within the wall. The Courier's head slowly rotated toward the display. One by one, a holographic bust appeared above each tree, each a different individual man or woman. "Each of these trees," said Lee, "is a kind of organic computer—all of the genius intellect without the tedious toil that slowed or burdened their human forms. Individually, without the distraction of morals, ethics, and emotions, they're incredibly powerful, but with the specialized mycelium linking them beneath the soil, they form an organic supercomputer. She'll be plugged into the mycelium network which will, as every other tree here has done, increase the power of the grove exponentially."

"There's a matter of payment," the Courier said, unimpressed. "The fee is the same."

Lee gazed at the Courier and sighed. His explanation and enthusiasm were obviously of no interest to the odd man sitting across the desk from him. "Of course," he said. Again, his fingers drummed across the embedded screen. "There we go. Payment in full."

From his inside pocket, the Courier withdrew a palm sized single pane viewer. Though only the back of the small transparent card was viewable from where Lee sat, the Courier's thick wide lenses reflected a few indecipherable lines of green text. After checking it, the Courier slipped the view card back into his inside pocket. "Contract complete," he said, then reached for the rock glass Lee had placed before him. "I'll have that drink." He swirled the whiskey, placed it under his meaty nose and inhaled deeply, flaring his nostrils, then quaffed it in one unceremonious gulp without a flinch or reaction to the strength of the alcohol. Lee's blue eyes widened in disbelief.

"Indeed," said the Courier. "That is good whiskey."

Disturbed by the wastefulness, Lee's response rolled out slow. "Yeeesss," he said.

The Courier set the glass back onto the surface of Lee's desk and ever so slightly smiled. "Time to start the next contract."

"That quick," Lee said with disinterest. Disappointed that the value of both his tree and whiskey were lost on the squat man, he grabbed the Courier's empty glass along with his own, rose from his chair, and with his back to Courier, returned to the shelved decanters.

"You'd be surprised," said the Courier. "The need for my services never seems to cease."

Lee glanced back, the Courier had already removed his spectacles and without them, his bulging bug eyes appeared ready to fall from the sockets. "I'm sure," Lee said, returning his attention to the shelf. "Your...services...are indeed unique." He poured a finger of whiskey into his glass, hesitated for a second, then poured another. He spun around to find the respirator already back on the bald man's head, the

Courier adjusting the straps above and below his wingnut ears. His voice muffled, the Courier continued, "The new contract came in from off-world."

"How exciting," said Lee, anticipating his guest's departure. "Off-world."

The Courier slipped his goggles on next, and then covered the hideous scars on his naked pate with his black fedora.

Lee swirled his spirits and sniffed from the glass. Despite the Courier, it was good whiskey. Then Lee's brow furrowed. "How can you take a job off-world without lace?"

"Oh," said the Courier beneath his respirator. "The contract came in from off-world. It's a standing strike-back."

"A strike-back?"

"Yes, it's a type of insurance policy that goes into effect after an anticipated action or incident. This particular subclass of insurance is called a strike-back."

"A retaliation," said Lee, pleased with the new topic. "And from off-world. How interesting. May I ask what does this one require?"

"All contracts are confidential."

"Of course."

"Under normal circumstances, but in this case, I can and will share it with you as I believe you will find it of great interest."

"I'm intrigued," Lee said, approaching the desk.

"You are correct that," the Courier continued, "apart from a sleeper ship, I cannot travel off-world without the necessary lacework implant. But this contract, like any other is for local execution."

"I see. Yes. That makes sense. So an accident happens—"

"No accident, something anticipated."

"Okay. Something anticipated happens, you automatically receive a contract."

"Automatically."

"Fascinating." Lee rested back into his chair, his cerulean eyes a near sparkle. "Yes I do find the..." his head wobbled as he searched for the word, "protocol, yes the protocol fascinating."

"As mentioned, I believe you will find this contract of great interest."

"And why is that?"

"This new contract was from the scientist."

"The scientist?" asked Lee.

"Yes. The one in the tree, Doctor Kim Yoo."

Lee's face went blank. "From Doctor Yoo?"

"Yes. She suspected that she may be in danger. Due to this, she requested that upon her death from the anticipated action or incident, a contract would go into effect."

Lee's glass slowly lowered to his lap. "What kind of contract did she arrange?"

"Same as any other. I am the Courier."

The fish eyed lenses of his goggles glowed tangerine.

"She wanted me to send you a message."

ABOUT THE AUTHORS

Ernie Howard was born on January 29,1977 during a Minnesota blizzard. His two story telling parents almost didn't make it to the hospital in their beat up blue Cadillac. Ernie is the writer of ***Write Something!,*** a book about the illusion of Writers Block. ***A World Without***, a Science Fiction book about the love between a husband and wife, and the darkness that can come into a marriage. ***Walter***, A Science Fiction book about a boy who is an outcast who makes a friend with a man that speaks to him through his television. Ernie lives with his wife and 3 boys in Henderson, NV, where he dreams up new stories, and tries to live everyday to the fullest.

Liviu Surugiu is a writer from outside the English-speaking world.

He is editor for the foreign stories in the Romanian magazine *CSF Magazine.*

Among his recent achievements, his prose was selected by The Lunar Codex project in NASA's Artemis program to be taken to the Polaris time capsule that will be buried by the Astrobotic Griffin / VIPER rover on the Moon next year.

On the Earth, his fiction has appeared in *Galaxy's Edge by Mike Resnick (US), Cirsova Magazine (US), Vigyan Katha (India), Galaktika (Hungary), Unfit Magazine (US), Orion's Belt Magazine (US), Gravity City (US), Supersonic (Spain), Nova Sci Fi Magazine (Germany), Teoria Omicron (Ecuador), Maquina Combinatoria (Peru), Algernon Magazine (Estonia), Short Edition (France),* and, of course, in the most important magazines and anthologies in Romania.

He received six Honorable Mention and two Silver HM from *Writers of the Future.* As a Romanian science fiction author, he won forty-one different awards over a thirty years career. Other awards he has received include: Second Place in the *HBO Screenwriter's Contest (2013), Best Novel of the Year 2015, Best Novel of the Year 2016, Best Short Story Collection 2016, Best Short Story of 2017, Best Story 2020, Best Short Story Collection 2022.* He also published eight books in Romania over the past eight years.

Steve Oden has worked in the publishing industry– mainly newspapers and magazines–for more than 30 years. Although retired, he provides editorial services on a consulting basis, mainly to corporate clients, and writes on assignment. His newspaper columns have appeared regularly in Tennessee and Alabama publications since 1980, winning awards from the Alabama Press Association, University of Tennessee-Tennessee Press Association, Society of Professional Journalists, National Rural Electric Cooperative Association and several wildlife conservation organizations.

Lara Frater published a non-fiction book *Fat Chicks Rule! How to Survive a Thin Centric World*. It was a guidebook on being a big girl in a thin world and included information on how to fat positive books, movies, and TV, where to find fashion, comfortable seating, and how to deal with fat hatred. A few months after the book was published, I did a companion blog with the same name that she still updates every Monday.

She has published essays, poetry and short stories.

In 2012, she published *End of the Line* the first in the series of three zombie novels that take place in a world almost dead of the flu and having to deal the zombies who rose from the ashes. *End of the Line* was followed by *Stuck in the Middle* in 2013 and *Full Circle* in 2014.

She is also working on a three book dystopian series called *Welcome to Pluto*. I hope to have the first book out in 2016.

She lives in New York City with her husband, author Jonathan Frater and has lots of animals and people in her house.

Jessica West (a.k.a. West1Jess) is currently pursuing a state of self-induced psychosis, also known as writing. In the past, she has worked for Wal-Mart, a lawyer, and a bank. Now if she could just get a couple years experience with the IRS and the NSA, world domination is in the bag.

Jess lives in Acadiana with three daughters still young enough to think she's cool and a husband who knows better but likes her anyway.

Daniel Arthur Smith is a USA Today bestselling author. His titles include *Spectral Shift*, *Hugh Howey Lives*, *The Cathari Treasure*, *The Somali Deception*, and a few other novels and short stories. He also curates the phenomenal short fiction series *Tales from the Canyons of the Damned* and *Frontiers of Speculative Fiction*.

He was raised in Michigan and graduated from Western Michigan University where he studied philosophy, with focus on cognitive science, meta-physics, and comparative religion. He began his career as a bartender, barista, poetry house proprietor, teacher, and then became a technologist and futurist for the Fortune 100 across the Americas and Europe.

Daniel has traveled to over 300 cities in 22 countries, residing in Los Angeles, Kalamazoo, Prague, Crete, and now writes in Manhattan where he lives with his wife and young sons.

For news and updates visit danielarthursmith.com